ADVENTURE TIME ™

It's a SLAMACOWTASTIC Story Mix-Up

Mr. Cupcake seems a little confused and needs your help telling the
most epic story he knows. Maybe he has just had too much sugar . . .
or not enough. Match the colored stickers with the missing words
in the story to help him along. Then use the other stickers to
create awesome scenes that go along with the story.

PSS!
Price Stern Sloan
An Imprint of Penguin Group (USA) Inc.

The publisher does not have any control over and does not assume
any responsibility for author or third-party websites or their content.

ADVENTURE TIME, CARTOON NETWORK, the logos, and all related
characters and elements are trademarks of and © Cartoon Network. (s12)

Published by Price Stern Sloan, a division of Penguin Young Readers Group, 345 Hudson Street,
New York, New York 10014. *PSS!* is a registered trademark of Penguin Group (USA) Inc. Printed in the U.S.A.

ISBN 978-0-8431-7222-5

10 9 8 7 6 5 4 3 2 1

ALWAYS LEARNING

PEARSON

P9-DCS-157

You think you're pretty kick butt , don't you?
Well, I bet you've never heard about the time
Finn and Jake had
to save Candy Kingdom from the evil clutches of
Ice King .

Like all epic stories, it began with a princess.
Princess Bubblegum was the most beautiful of all
the princesses and Ice King wanted her
to be his bride.

This princess was at a princess Science Dance with all the other princesses. They were dancing, singing, and having an all-around algebraic time.

From the shadows came Ice King and his sinister team of little tuxedo people .
Before the other princesses knew what had happened, Ice King captured Princess Bubblegum and took her back to his kingdom.

Finn and **Jake** were poking around in a pile of junk when they heard the princess calling for help.

These two **heroes** craved adventure—it was their favorite time of day. They jumped to action and charged forth to rescue **Princess Bubblegum**.

In true ninja style, **Finn** and **Jake** made their way to the lair of the mean **Ice King** .

Along the way, they ran into **Marceline** , who warned them that true **ninjas** can sense the intentions of their enemies.

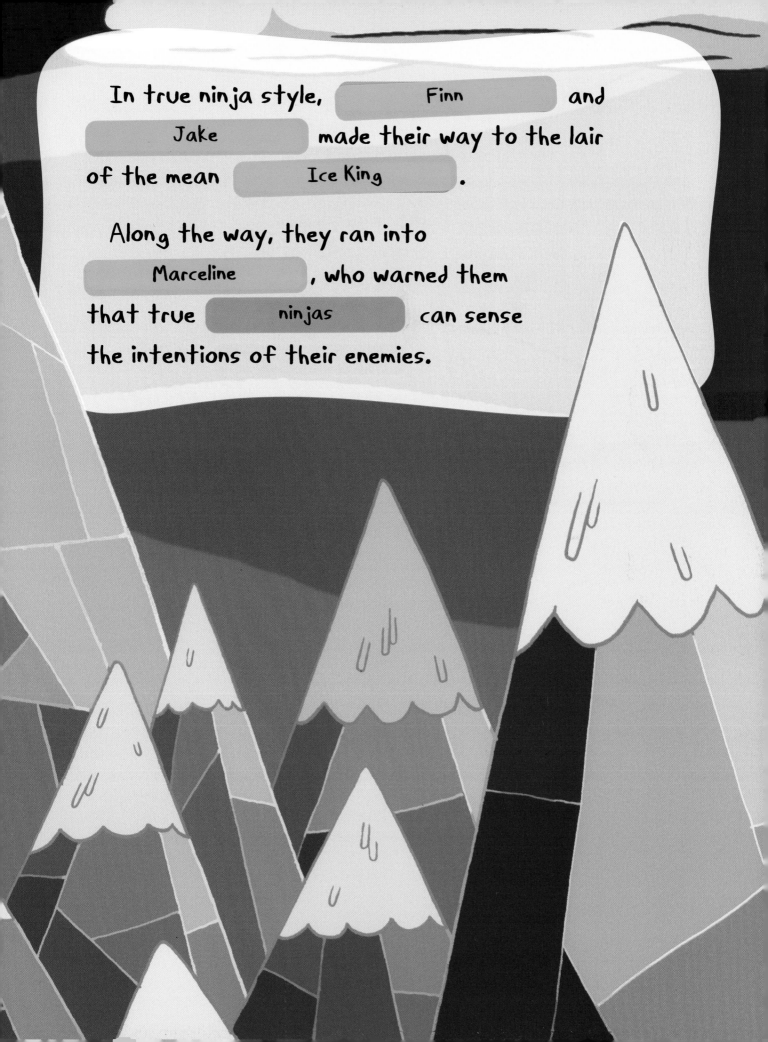

The battle was [kick butt] . There was ninja fighting all over the place. [Finn] and [Jake] punched, kicked, and trash-talked [Ice King] right in his face.

[Ice King] tried to fight back, but then [Finn] kicked him so hard that he left the planet—taking his loyal [little tuxedo people] with him.

Mathematical!

Ice King and the little tuxedo people found themselves floating through space. It probably wasn't so bad for ICE KING. Space has its own princess . . . and I hear that she's very lumpy.

And there you have it. The greatest story you never heard. Can you believe that Finn and Jake did all those awesome things? I sure can't . . . and I was there. Wasn't I?

	Princess Bubblegum	Lumpy Space Princess
	Princess Bubblegum	Lumpy Space Princess
	Princess Bubblegum	Lady Rainicorn
		Lady Rainicorn
	Marceline	Lady Rainicorn
	Marceline	Peanut Princess
	Marceline	Skeleton Princess
	BMO	Tree Trunks
	BMO	Tree Trunks
	BMO	Turtle Princess
	BMO	Wildberry Princess
	BMO	Gunter
		Gunter
		Gunter
		Gunter
Jake		Candy People
		Candy People
		Candy People
Princess Bubblegum		
Princess Bubblegum	Lumpy Space Princess	heroes

™ & © Cartoon Network. (s12)

™ & © Cartoon Network. (s12)

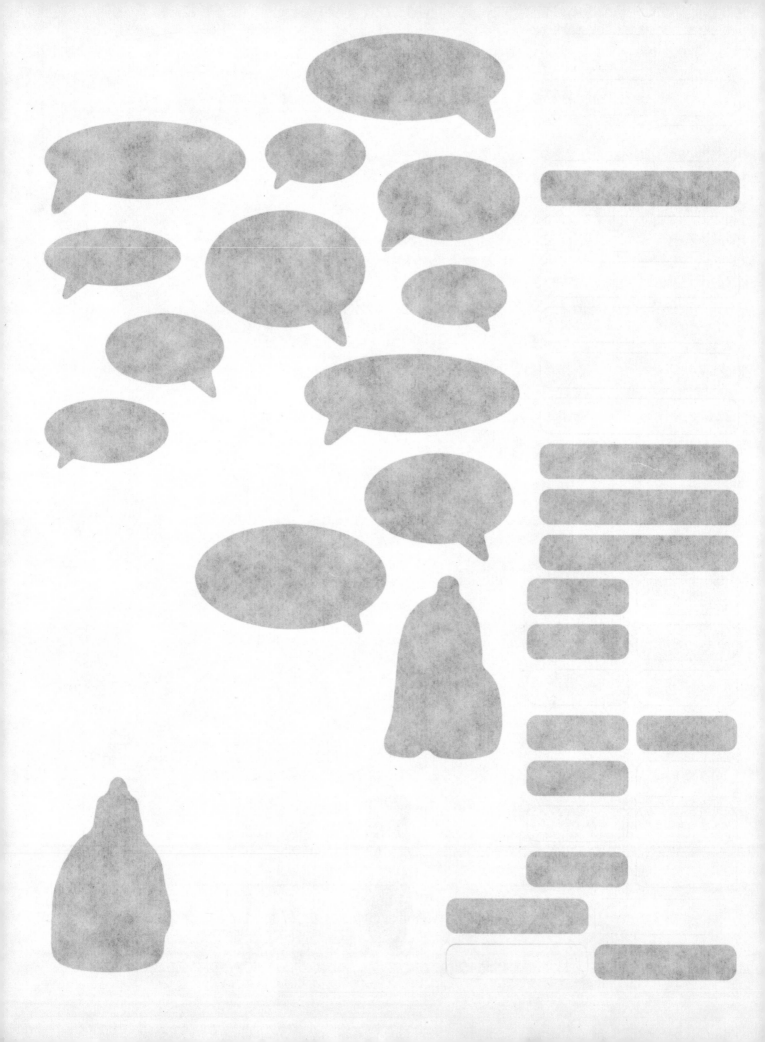

™ & © Cartoon Network. (s12)

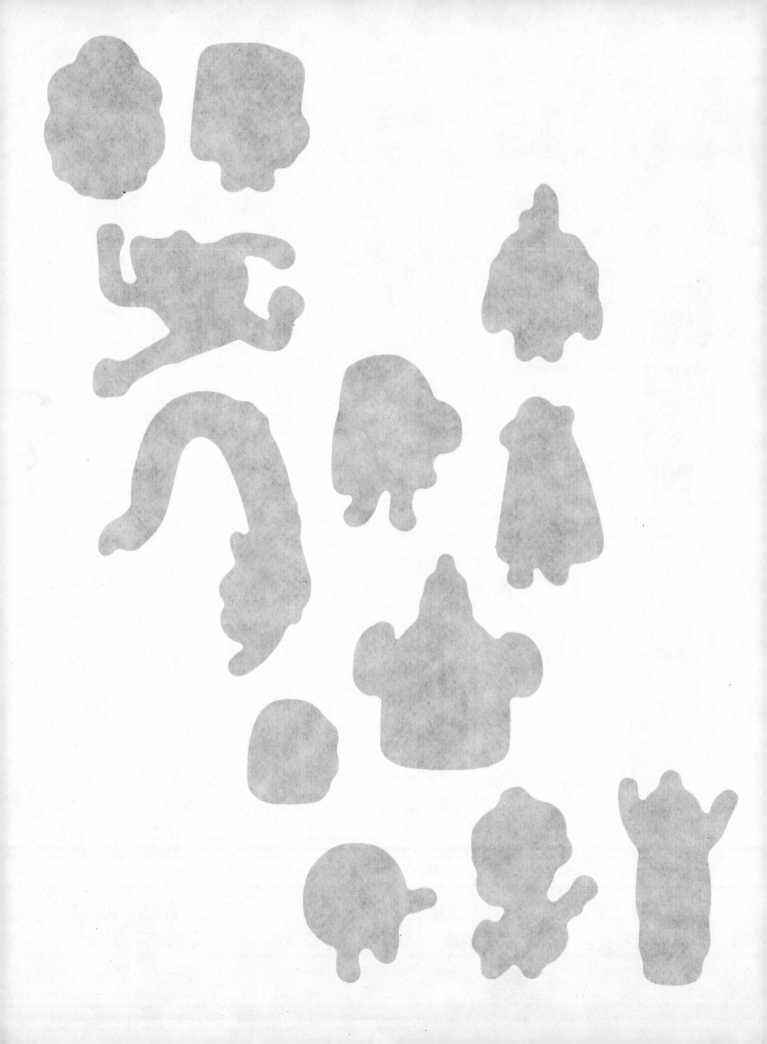

™ & © Cartoon Network. (s12)

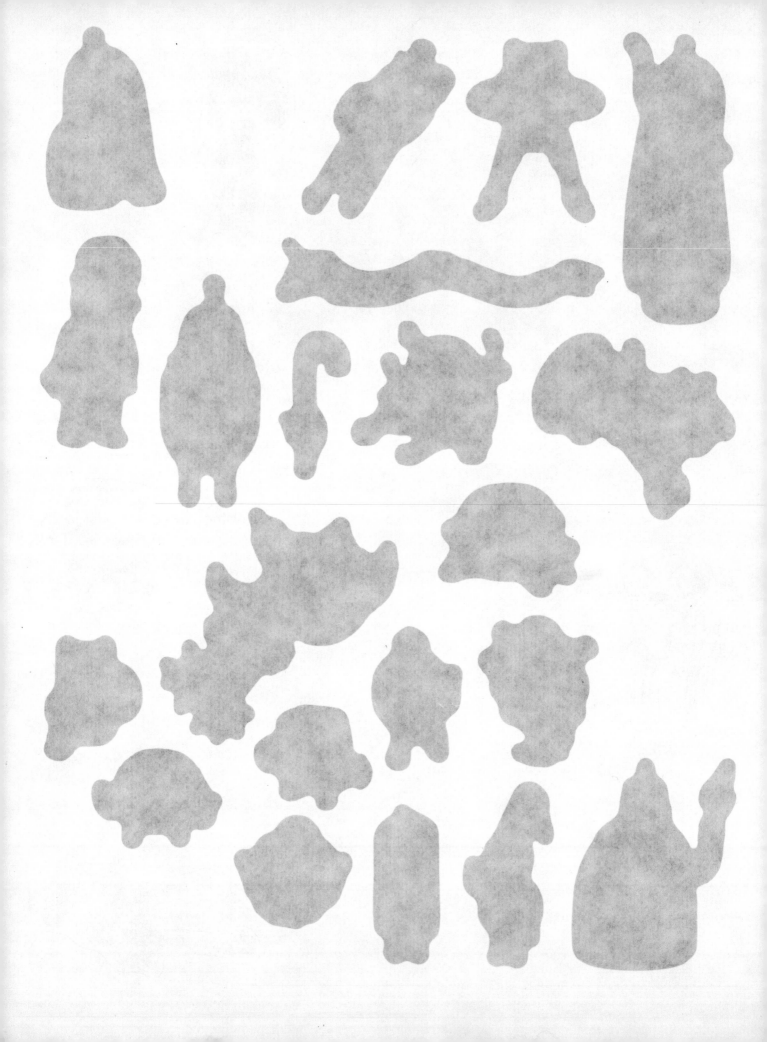